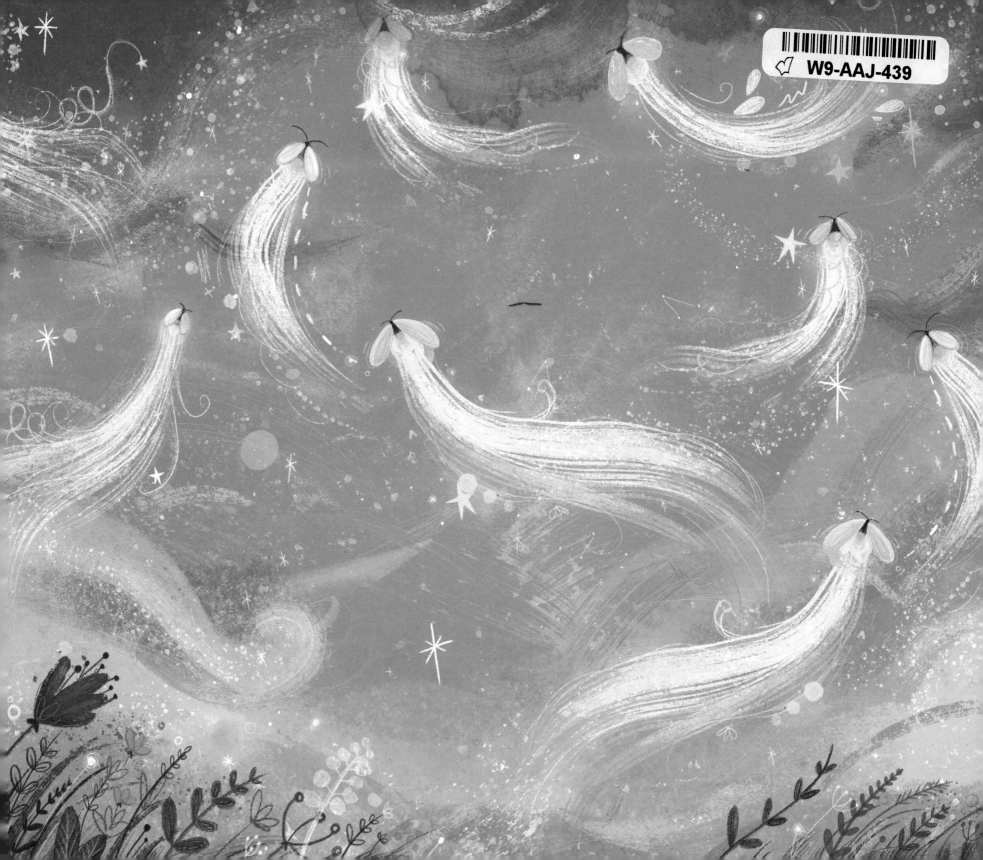
W9-AAJ-439

Friends of the
Lancaster Public Library

Donated By

In memory of:
Joe Foshaski

For Ayden and Baby Vigilance
–LD

For Leo and Cameo
–LF

ZONDERKIDZ

Stay This Way Forever
Copyright © 2021 by Linsey Davis
Illustrations © 2021 by Lucy Fleming

Requests for information should be addressed to:

Zonderkidz, 3900 Sparks Drive, Grand Rapids, Michigan 49546

Library of Congress Control Number: 2020943026
Hardcover ISBN 978-0-310-77008-4
Ebook ISBN 978-0-310-77009-1

All Scripture quotations, unless otherwise indicated, are taken from The Holy Bible,
New International Version®, NIV®. Copyright © 1973, 1978, 1984, 2011 by Biblica, Inc.® Used by permission.
All rights reserved worldwide.

Any internet addresses (websites, blogs, etc.) and telephone numbers in this book are offered as a resource.
They are not intended in any way to be or imply an endorsement by Zondervan, nor does
Zondervan vouch for the content of these sites and numbers for the life of this book.

No part of this publication may be reproduced, stored in a retrieval system, or transmitted
in any form or by any means—electronic, mechanical, photocopy, recording, or any other—
except for brief quotations in printed reviews, without the prior permission of the publisher.

Zonderkidz is a trademark of Zondervan.

Content Contributor: Barbara Herndon

Design and art direction: *Kris Nelson/StoryLook Design*

Printed in Korea

21 22 23 24 25 / SHW / 21 20 19 18 17 16 15 14 13 12 11 10 9 8 7 6 5 4 3 2 1

Stay This Way Forever

Written by
LINSEY DAVIS

Illustrated by Lucy Fleming

LANCASTER PUBLIC LIBRARY
LANCASTER, PA

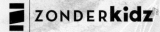
ZONDERkidz

The sleepy sun is setting, and another day is done.
The lightning bugs have dimmed their lights and bedtime has begun.

The moment that you're tucked in tight and you drift off to sleep,
I think of all the memories that I would like to keep.

Your joyful songs, your belly laughs, the clever things you say,
Are moments from this fairy tale I cherish every day.
Like footprints tracked along the shore, or flower blooms in May,
I try to memorize those times before they slip away.

I'll hold them close, like I hold you—pressed against my heart—
And marvel at the child you are as every new day starts.

You wake up every morning with a grin from ear to ear,
Then wrap your arms around my neck ... your snuggles are so dear.
You pucker up for kisses, unafraid to let love show.
The feeling is pure joy each time I hear your sweet "Hello!"

Your giggles make ME giggle as we share a tickle fight.
You catch your breath then start to squeal—the sound is pure delight!
Sweet child, keep the love and joy in everything you do.

STAY THIS WAY FOREVER
is the wish I have for you.

You're curious about the world and everything you see.
From dew drops on a flower to the buzzing of a bee.
I'm inspired every day to see things through your eyes,
Reminding me the world is filled with wonder and surprise.

Your innocent and open heart sees only what is good.

I hope you STAY THIS WAY FOREVER, long past childhood.

Each day I watch you build the most imaginary things,
Like castles made for unicorns ...

... and rocket ships with wings.

Always keep creating—let that side of you run wild.
So when you find you're all grown up you'll still dream like a child.

When music plays, you're dancing—wiggling, jiggling to the beat.

My heart smiles as you close your eyes and move your happy feet.

My dream is that you'll STAY THIS WAY FOREVER and a day

And dance in celebration of your life along the way.

When you're hurt or feeling bad, I wipe away your tears,
Then cuddle close and hold you tight to soothe away your fears.
There might be days when things get tough and you just want to hide.
But please remember this, my love, I'll be right by your side.

I'll always be there watching, trying to keep you safe from harm.

You'll never be too big for me to hold you in my arms.

I have so many dreams for you and what your life may hold.
I'm blessed to have a front row seat to watch it all unfold.

But for now, please promise me, as you begin to grow,
That you'll stay true to who you are and everything you know.

Whether you are three years old or even eighty-three,
Find the feeling in your soul that keeps you wild and free.

Fill the world with laughter as you skip and dance and spin,
And keep your big heart open wide so love comes rushing in.

Create and find the WONDERFUL in everything you do always knowing ... and STAY THIS WAY FOREVER

I love you.